The Nocturnal Adventures of Anna the Hamster

Written by Louise Speaight

Illustrated by Lynsey Hooper

© Louise Speaight 2022

To my family

For always giving in to my pleas for childhood pets
and fuelling my imagination through reading.

Chapter 1 – Home

The Study is the second place that Anna has called home. This is quite impressive considering that Anna is only three months old, which does not seem old at all, until you realise that she is about the same age as you in human years.

With sunshine yellow walls displaying smiling photographs of the big people she lives with and floral curtains framing the view out of the window to the village pond, The Study was a place where Anna felt safe and content. Hamsters are nocturnal creatures, sleeping in the day and awake at night, so The Study, being the quietest room in the house, was the perfect home for Anna. Her cage sat on top of an antique dresser, which was far enough away from the desk where the big people occasionally worked that Anna could get plenty of sleep. More importantly, Anna's cage was close enough to the window so that when she was running in her wheel at night, Anna could see the stars twinkling and watch the other nocturnal animals going about their lives.

"Oh what it would be like to be able to fly," thought Anna out loud to herself whilst looking out of the window into the night. "The bats and the owls dart through the sky so freely. The places they must be able to visit in just one night!"

Imagining the world outside of her window got Anna thinking about her early life in The Pet Shop. The Pet Shop was her first home where she had grown up with her six brothers and four sisters. Each morning, as dawn was breaking, they used

to snuggle up together in their nest whilst Mother would share amazing bedtime stories of her childhood growing up in Russia. These were Anna's fondest memories.

Anna loved drifting off to sleep imagining playing in the wheat fields of Siberia - just like her Mother had done. Mother had told her that Siberia was a very cold, harsh place to grow up, especially in the Winter. Mother and Anna's grandparents used to pride themselves on their snug underground burrow, which kept them warm on the coldest of Winter days. Mother shared stories of how she helped to make their nest extra cosy by collecting and lining it with animal fur or wool that she found in the forest nearby. When the Sun did come out in Siberia and the wheat grew, they had to work hard to collect as many grains as they could – filling their cheeks to the brim to take back and store in their underground burrow. This made sure that they had plenty of food to last them through Winter. It was not all work though. Mother had also told Anna stories of how she had raced to climb to the top of the tallest wheat grass in the field, being careful that the owls did not spot her. The climb and the danger were worth it – from the top of the wheat grass Mother said you could see far and wide, into the forest which ran alongside their field and all the way to the huge snow topped mountains in the distance. Anna dreamed that one day she too could experience such an adventure! She loved her home in The Study, she enjoyed running around in her wheel and prided herself in keeping a fluffy, cosy nest, but she longed to travel as Mother had done. She too wanted to experience the freedom of the other nocturnal creatures outside of The Study window. Anna knew that there was a whole exciting world out there, but she just did not know how to get out of her cage to see it! The big people were always careful to close the door on the top of her cage securely and the bars were too narrow to squeeze through and too strong to bite through. "My only hope is that one day the smaller of the big people will forget to shut my cage door properly after giving me a cuddle," pondered Anna out loud whilst yet again testing that the door was indeed firmly shut to her cage. "Then I'll head out for adventure and never look back!"

Chapter 2 – A Visitor

Day turned to night and night turned to day and Anna continued to dream of adventure. When one of the smaller of the big people did wake her up for a cuddle, Anna would first get a buzz of excitement with the anticipation that this time they would forget to shut her cage door securely, only to then feel disappointment when they did not. To take her mind off things, she contented herself with running around in her wheel all night. It was during one of her runs, in which Anna was having a particularly exciting daydream of climbing to the top of the tallest wheat grass in the field, when something interrupted her. She stopped running, slowed the wheel to a halt, and listened. There it was again. A faint knock on her cage door. Anna jumped off her wheel so that she could see the door on the roof of her cage. To her amazement, the source of the knocking was a field mouse! He looked exactly like Anna – they both had lovely golden-brown coats of fur with white underbellies. The only difference was that he had a long pink tail – nearly as long as his body! Anna had always wondered what it would be like to have a tail ... hamsters do not have them you see.

Seeing that he had got Anna's attention, he knocked again and said "Hello neighbour. My name's Douglas and I live in the walls of the house. I'm sorry to interrupt your run, however I'm in a bit of a dilemma." "It's lovely to meet you Douglas," said Anna reaching her little pink paw through the cage bars so that she could shake Douglas' little pink paw. "I'm Anna. I had no idea that I had a neighbour! What is your dilemma? I'd be happy to help in any way I can." "That's very kind of you Anna," continued Douglas, "you see, the big people have put down some mouse traps around my hole in the kitchen wall and I'm now unable to get to my beloved cheese! There is a lovely wheel of cheddar sitting on top of the kitchen counter – I can smell it, but I just cannot get to it! I have not eaten since breakfast yesterday evening and I am getting quite hungry! I was wondering if you would be kind enough to allow me to borrow some of your grains? I'll of course repay you when I find a way around the mouse traps."

"Oh, you poor thing," sighed Anna, "that is a dilemma! I've got plenty of grains, and besides, it's nearly morning, so the big people will fill my bowl up again when they come down for their breakfast." Anna imagined that she would need to pass her grains through the bars to Douglas, however, much to her amazement, Douglas proceeded to open the door to Anna's cage! Anna watched in wonder as he slowly climbed down inside, holding tightly onto the bars, and taking great care not to fall. Field mice are great climbers, just like hamsters, however Douglas had never been in a cage before, and the steel bars were a little slippery. “You can open my cage door,” marvelled Anna, “I’ve been longing to be able to get out.”

“Why is that?” asked Douglas, “you have got a lovely home,” he admired as he looked around. Anna had a kitchen where her food bowl and water bottle sat, her running wheel and a huge, lovely, snug looking bed which was made from fluffed up wood pulp and paper. “Thank you,” said Anna. “The big people take incredibly good care of me and I particularly love my view out of the window. But my cage is quite small, and I would love to get out and explore the world. I’ve just never been able to open the door from the inside! I have also never had a visitor before. Do make yourself comfortable on the wood pulp in my kitchen and please help yourself to as many grains as you need.”

Douglas was incredibly grateful to Anna as he sat down and started eating. “I’m sorry that I’ve not visited you before now,” he admitted. “I’ve been living behind the house walls for about a year. I love living here. I can roam from room to room behind the walls and even access the garden via the drainpipes. The garden visits are my favourite outings – I use the drainpipes like giant slides and land on the soft grass at the bottom. It is such fun! I can show you sometime if you'd like?"

Anna did not need time to think about her answer. She finally had a way out of her cage and an invitation for adventure! She was so excited by the prospect that she was jumping up and down on the spot when she exclaimed to Douglas "Oh yes, yes please! I have been waiting for the moment I can get out and see the world, just like my Mother had done. How incredibly exciting!" "Well, that's settled then," Douglas laughed as he stood up, belly full. "I'll come back this evening at midnight when all of the big people are fast asleep, and I'll give you a tour of the house." With that, Douglas started to make the climb back up the side of Anna's cage. Being a great climber, he had already got used to clinging to the steel bars, so he went less carefully this time. He shut the cage door, thanked Anna again for her hospitality and bid her farewell until midnight.

Even though dawn was starting to break, Anna was far too excited to sleep. Adventure was waiting and she had a new friend to experience it with. To tire herself out, she decided to set about cleaning and fluffing up her already huge bed. She built up the wood pulp and paper to form a cosy nest to sleep in – Mother would have approved. Anna was snuggling down to sleep just as the big people were coming down for their breakfast and to refill her food bowl with grains. She slept deeply all day, dreaming of walking through one of Douglas' holes and into the thrilling unknown behind the wall.

Chapter 3 – The Adventure Begins

Anna rose from bed at seven o'clock in the evening after a much-needed sleep. She ate her breakfast and had a wash using the water from her water bottle. She also got to have a cuddle with one of the smaller of the big people before they went up to bed, but by eight o'clock she was restless. She kept looking at the dials on the clock on the wall of The Study. Midnight was coming around so slowly! It seemed like time was standing still. By ten thirty, when all the big people were tucked up in bed, Anna decided to go for a run in her wheel to take her mind off watching the clock. The rhythm of the wheel going around and around under Anna's tiny pink feet helped to pass the time. She lost herself in the view outside of The Study window. Around and around she ran whilst watching the bats flying and listening to the owls hooting. She quite forgot about the clock until she heard the knock on her cage door. Anna slammed on her brakes, leapt off her wheel, which was quite a feat as it was still spinning, and looked up to see Douglas smiling down at her. "Good evening Anna," said Douglas merrily, "I hope you are still ready for an adventure?" "I was born ready!" exclaimed Anna, jumping up and down on the spot in excitement. Her long run had clearly not tired her out. "I'll be straight up," she continued. She stopped for a quick drink from her water bottle and to store grains in both of her cheeks for Douglas to eat later. With that, she proceeded to climb up the steel bars of her cage to meet Douglas at the top where he had already opened the door for her. What a thrill, she was finally out of her cage!

In all her excitement, Anna still remembered the reason she had been given this opportunity for adventure. “If the mouse traps are still in the kitchen, I’ve brought some more grains for you,” she said in a somewhat muffled voice as her cheeks were so full. “Unfortunately yes, the traps are still there, so that’s very thoughtful of you,” sighed Douglas. He pointed at the hole in the skirting board underneath the big people’s desk. “We will go through the wall and start our adventure on the first floor tonight. I can show you my home and you can drop off the grains that you’ve kindly brought along for me.” With that, they climbed down the side of Anna’s cage, jumping up onto and along the window ledge. There was then a little hop onto the top of the desk followed by a careful climb down the knobs on the desk draws until they reached the floor underneath. There they disappeared through the hole in the skirting board. Anna did not once hesitate or look back – she was just so happy!

If you are one of the big people, and indeed, even if you are one of the smaller of the big people, there is absolutely no room for you behind the walls of a house. For little hamsters and field mice however, the walls seem to open like a huge cave that stretches up and up towards the top of the house – much further than Anna could see. There was a maze of wooden beams which Douglas referred to as their paths. Going off in all directions he explained that they would take them anywhere that they wanted to go in the house. “We are going to take this path here,” said Douglas leading Anna through the maze, “this one takes us straight to my home.” They zig-zagged up and up the beams until they reached the first floor. There, in the wall which backed onto the airing cupboard beyond, Douglas had made a cosy little nest of cotton wool for himself. “In the Winter, my home is lovely and warm. The big people have the heating on and the heat from the boiler in the airing cupboard travels through this wall and warms my bed,” explained Douglas. “Your home is so lovely,” said Anna, “it must be so snug. I can see why you love living here.” She found a little nook next to Douglas’ nest and deposited the grains out of her cheeks. Thanking her again for her generosity, Douglas ate a couple of grains to stop his belly from rumbling – he had not, after all, eaten since he had visited Anna the night before. Once finished, he was ready to show her around.

"Come on Anna, let me introduce you to my other neighbour, Tilly."
Tilly the house spider lived just around the corner from Douglas where she had spun her web hanging in between two adjoining wooden beams. "Hello neighbour," said Douglas tugging on one of the threads of Tilly's web, so that she knew that he and Anna had come to visit. In response, Tilly scurried down the thread to meet them. "How lovely to see you Douglas, it's been far too long," she said hovering in her web just above their heads. "Yes, I apologise for not visiting sooner Tilly," explained Douglas, "but you see I've been having some difficulty getting to my beloved cheese. The big people have put mouse traps around my hole in the kitchen wall. Anna here has been feeding me until we can find a solution to the problem." "It's lovely to meet you Tilly," beamed Anna. "I've not met a spider before! What a grand home you've weaved for yourself." "Why thank you my dear," replied Tilly with a bow of her head, "it's lovely to meet you too. I take great care in weaving my web. It is especially important to me. As you see, it's both my bed and my kitchen." Looking around, Anna could see that Tilly did not have any worries with where her next meal was coming from. She had caught plenty of flies and wrapped them up in her web ready to eat. Tilly continued: "I'm sorry to hear about your troubles Douglas. Maybe Alexander, having experience with the ways of the big people, could help you to find a way

around the traps?" "Oh, I hadn't thought of that!" exclaimed Douglas excitedly, "I bet Alexander will know exactly what to do." It was getting late and Douglas needed to get Anna back home before the big people came down for their breakfast. "Anna if you are up for another adventure tomorrow night, I can introduce you to my good friend Alexander? For now though, we should move quickly. Dawn is breaking and we need to get you home before the big people come to refill your food bowl." "Oh, don't worry my dears," said Tilly casually, "I can get you back home in no time Anna."

She instantly went about spinning two new threads to her web, dangled them down and told Douglas and Anna to tie them around their waists.

“Don’t worry my lovelies, this is perfectly safe,” beamed Tilly proudly “my web is as strong as steel. Just step off the wooden beam and I will lower you both down to the ground floor. When you get there, tug on the thread once and I’ll let you go.” They both did as Tilly said, thanked her and, before they knew it, they had glided back down to the ground floor. They wearily made the climb back up to Anna’s cage on top of the antique dresser. Lowering herself through her cage door Anna said to Douglas “That was the best night of my life! I’ve had so much fun!” “Well, I’m incredibly pleased you enjoyed it Anna,” smiled Douglas “I’ll see you again this evening at midnight and I’ll take you to meet my good friend Alexander.” With that, he waved, turned, and climbed off to his bed. Anna was exhausted. She snuggled down into her nest and dreamed of Tilly and the world behind the walls.

Chapter 4 – Alexander the Great

Anna was so exhausted after her first adventure that she did not rise until after eight o'clock that evening. She was also very hungry – she had been far too excited to eat much the night before, so she very much enjoyed her breakfast whilst being mindful to keep enough grains aside for Douglas.

To reserve her energy, she decided that she would not run on her wheel tonight, but instead decided to use the fresh wood pulp and paper the big people had provided to extend her nest. She added a lovely little seating area where she rested. She happily contented herself with watching the nocturnal creatures who were again going about their lives outside of The Study window. Her mind started turning to what adventure she might have in store for tonight. Douglas had mentioned that he was going to take her to see his good friend Alexander. Who or what creature Alexander was Anna did not know, but if he was anything as friendly and as interesting as Tilly, then she was very much looking forward to meeting him.

True to his word and on-time, Douglas knocked on Anna's cage door at the stroke of midnight. Anna was ready and waiting for Douglas with her cheeks already filled with his grains. “I can’t thank you enough for sharing your food with me again Anna,” said Douglas. “Hopefully, a visit to Alexander tonight can help me to find a solution to these pesky mouse traps and I can get back to eating my beloved cheese.”

Remembering the way from last night, Anna set off after Douglas across the window ledge. She descended carefully down the knobs of the desk drawers, down underneath the desk and through the hole in the skirting board. They first visited Douglas’ nest so that Anna could deposit the grains. Then, shouting “hello” and waving to Tilly on the way past her web, they started the climb up to the loft. “Does Alexander live all the way up at the top of the house in the loft?” enquired Anna. “Well, it depends,” explained Douglas “Alexander doesn’t really have a home, he tends to wonder about the walls of the house, never staying in one place for very long. I had heard that he was enjoying the company of Mr and Mrs Blackbird, who are using the warm loft to hatch their chicks. I’m hoping that we aren’t too late, and we can catch up with him there before he heads on to another part of the house.”

It was a tiring climb all the way up to the loft, so Anna was pleased that she had decided against a run on her wheel this evening. The zig-zagging wooden beams seemed to go on and on forever until they finally reached the very top of the house.

Douglas spotted Mrs Blackbird sitting sleepily on her nest.

Looking at her, you would not obviously know that she was a Blackbird, after all, her feathers were brown! She did however have a beautiful bright yellow beak. As they moved closer to her, her eyes fluttered open. “Excuse me Mrs Blackbird, we are sorry to wake you,” said Douglas respectfully, “I’m Douglas and this is my friend Anna. We are searching for my incredibly good friend Alexander. Have you seen him recently by any chance?” “Hello little ones,” cooed Mrs Blackbird, “it’s quite alright. I was just taking the opportunity to doze off whilst my chicks are asleep. I believe that Alexander is talking to Mr Blackbird over there.” She pointed her bright yellow beak over their shoulders to an area just next to the big people’s suitcases. The loft was full to the brim of the big people’s belongings. Anna concluded that they must not use some of them very much as they were covered in a thick layer of dust!

Thanking Mrs Blackbird and leaving her to go back to sleep, they weaved in and out, over and under all the big people’s belongings until they finally reached Alexander and Mr Blackbird. Unlike his wife, Mr Blackbird had the most amazing jet-black feathers, which lived up to his name, but he shared the same beautiful bright yellow beak as Mrs Blackbird.

"Alexander!" cried Douglas drawing him in for a big hug "it's so great to see you again my good friend." "Douglas!" cried Alexander back, hugging Douglas extra tightly "it's been far too long!" Stepping apart to look at each other, but still embracing, Douglas said to Alexander "I've made a new friend since we last met. I'd like to introduce you to Anna." Walking forward, Alexander reached out a tiny pink paw "It's a pleasure to meet you Anna," he smiled. Forgetting all her manners, Anna stood motionless on the spot, just staring at Alexander. Douglas gave a little awkward cough which thankfully brought Anna back to her senses ... she reached out her tiny pink paw to shake his "But you're a ... I didn't realise that you are ... I wasn't expecting to meet ... a fellow hamster!" stuttered Anna in surprise. Alexander, as it turned out, was a Russian hamster just like Anna, however whereas her coat was a lovely golden-brown, Alexander's was a light grey with a dark grey stripe running from between his ears straight down along his back.

“Well, I have to say that I’m as surprised as you!” laughed Alexander, “You see, I’ve lived in your house for 9 months now. I used to call the house next door my home. I was there for just over a year when one of the smaller of the big people from my family took me out of my cage, put me in a plastic ball and carried me out to the garden. At first, I had such fun running freely around in my plastic ball over the grass. I enjoyed taking in all the new sights and smells. But after a while, I got a bit too carried away and started running a bit too quickly. Before I knew what was happening, I was rolling down a hill and straight into the hedgerow at the edge of the garden! The force of the impact caused my plastic ball to pop open and I flew into the middle of the hedge! I could hear the smaller of the big people crying my name and searching for me, but with the tall bushes all around me, I could not find a way out! I am not sure how long I was walking until I finally made it out of the hedgerow. It turns out that days had passed, and it was nightfall. I could hear the creatures of the night all around me, so I ran as quickly as I could across the garden back towards the house. It was only then that I realised that this was not my house! I had no choice but to climb all the way up one of the drainpipes and into the loft. I met Mr and Mrs Blackbird and they were very welcoming. They said that there was plenty of room for me to make this house my home, so I started roaming the walls and making friends with all the creatures who already lived here. That's how I met Douglas."

"Wow what a life you lead," marvelled Anna, "you must have such amazing stories to share. This is only my second ever adventure. I live in The Study downstairs. Douglas kindly opened my cage door for me, so that I could help him to get back to his beloved cheese." "Is this what brings you up to the loft Douglas?" questioned Alexander "If so, how can I help you dear friend?"

Douglas explained the mouse traps to Alexander and about Anna kindly sharing her grains. He said that Tilly had suggested, with his experience of living with the big people next door, that Alexander might be able to help them to devise a plan to get to his beloved cheese. Alexander was giving all this some careful thought when, clearing his throat, Mr Blackbird stepped forward and cooed: "I hope you don't mind; however, I've been listening to your problem and I might just have an idea!" Mr Blackbird went on to explain that on his many flights beyond the garden hedgerow, he often sang out good morning to Bertie the woodpecker. "Strange fellow is Bertie," bemused Mr Blackbird. "He much prefers pecking away at a tree to get to the beetle grubs beneath the bark, rather than catching flies on the wing like Mrs Blackbird and I do. Anyway, he is an expert at pecking holes through wood. I bet he could easily peck a new hole in the kitchen wall, so that you can get to your cheese! I'm sure if you asked him nicely, he would do this for you one evening in exchange for some of Anna's grains."

"Why that's a brilliant idea!" exclaimed Alexander, Douglas, and Anna in unison. Alexander thought some more and continued: "If Bertie was kind enough to peck you a hole high up in the kitchen ceiling Douglas, then the big people couldn't put any more traps in your way!" "That's all very well," thought Douglas out loud, "but how would I get from the new hole to the kitchen counter where the cheese is kept?" "That's easy," explained Anna. "When we met Tilly yesterday, she proudly told us that the threads of her web are as strong as steel. If she can lower each of us to the ground floor on a single thread, I am sure that she could easily build you a bridge between the new hole and the kitchen counter. This would provide you with your own private pathway directly to your beloved cheese."

"Ingenious! What a great plan." marvelled Douglas. "Thank you, friends. There is only one problem ... where do we find Bertie and how do we get to him? As Alexander knows from experience, the garden is a huge place – it's a hazardous journey for us to make." "No problem," said Mr Blackbird, "I'll see Bertie on my flight tomorrow. I'll ask him to meet you by the edge of the patio at one o'clock tomorrow morning, next to the bright blue pot with the yellow daffodils in it." And just like that the plan was set. They all called it a night and went off to their beds to get plenty of rest – every one of them dreaming about the adventure they had in store.

Chapter 5 – Down the Drainpipe

Again, at the stroke of midnight, Anna was ready and waiting for Douglas. She had eaten her breakfast and stored Douglas' grains in her cheeks. They set off along the window ledge, carefully down the knobs of the desk draws, underneath the desk, and through the hole in the skirting board. As with last night's adventure, the first stop was Douglas' nest where Anna deposited his grains. "As always, thank you so much for sharing your food with me Anna," said Douglas smiling, "hopefully this will be the last time you have to if we pull off our plan!"

Before setting off to the loft where Alexander was waiting for them, they first stopped to visit Tilly so that they could share their plan with her. "Oh, how wonderfully exciting my dears!" exclaimed Tilly once they had told her about Bertie. "Of course, I can build you a bridge Douglas, it's no bother at all. I'll make sure I reserve plenty of my energy tonight so that I can produce my strongest threads for you tomorrow." Thanking her they turned and started their long climb up to the loft, zigzagging along the pathways of the wooden beams until they eventually reached it.

“Good evening Mr and Mrs Blackbird, Alexander” both Anna and Douglas squeaked, “did everything go as planned today Mr Blackbird?” “Why certainly, cooed Mr Blackbird, “I met Bertie on my dawn flight and he’s happy to meet you next to the bright blue pot with the yellow daffodils at one o’clock.” As if reminding them of the time, at that moment, the large grandfather clock in the hallway of the house chimed half past midnight. “That is in half an hours’ time!” panicked Anna, “we need to get going!” “Don’t worry Anna,” reassured Douglas, “we are taking the shortcut down to the garden. Remember I told you about my favourite thing to do in the house? We are going to use the drainpipes like giant slides! These will take us all the way to the garden where we will land on the soft grass below.” “What a thrill!” beamed Anna, jumping up and down on the spot in excitement. “It certainly is,” smiled Alexander, “let us use that drainpipe over there. It is the one closest to the corner of the patio where we are meeting Bertie. It will still require a short walk, but we should be on time to meet him at one o’clock, as agreed.”

Alexander went into the drainpipe first. Anna could hear him shout “weeeeeeeee!!!” as he slid all the way down the pipe and into the garden. Douglas agreed to go last in case there were any problems, so it was Anna’s turn next. Douglas instructed her to keep her little pink paws crossed over her chest and her tiny pink feet together, to avoid any potential issues of getting stuck! She sat on the lip of the pipe, gave herself a little push, and off she went! She could not help herself “weeeeeeeee!!!” she shouted as she shot down the pipe. The fact that the inside of the drainpipe was dark just added to the excitement. Before she knew it, Anna was bursting out of the pipe and into the soft garden grass. “Oh, I’d love to do that again,” exclaimed Anna standing up “that was so much fun!” Douglas landed in the grass next to her, picked himself up and the three companions made the short walk over towards the daffodil pot.

They had only been waiting a little time when they saw Bertie making his descent down to them in the moonlight. Bertie was a green feathered woodpecker with a brilliant red marking on top of his head. He also had black patches over his white eyes, which looked a bit like a mask. “Good evening,” he cawed. “Do I have the pleasure of meeting Douglas?” “It’s lovely to meet you Bertie,” replied Douglas. “I’d like to introduce you to my good friends Alexander and Anna. I’m so grateful that you’ve offered to help me.” The introductions were made, and the payment of grains was agreed. Anna offered to bring them to Bertie the following night, so that she could ride the drainpipe slide once again. They were just about to set off back across the patio towards the house when a shadow swooped past them overhead.

“What was that?” whispered Alexander. Anna thought about it and concluded: “It was either a bat or an owl. I see them most nights out of The Study window. We need to be careful of the owls. I remember Mother telling me stories of the owls hunting in the wheat fields of Siberia. You need to keep hidden in amongst the wheat otherwise they will carry you off to their nest!” “Oh poppycock!” dismissed Douglas. “This isn’t a wheat field in Siberia, but a country garden in England.” With that he strode off confidently on his own back across the patio towards the house. The others were just about to follow behind him when the shadow passed again overhead. They heard the beating of wings and a squeak from Douglas as the owl grabbed him in her talons and lifted him off into the air!

All Anna and Alexander could do was watch helplessly, but thankfully Bertie jumped into action. He soared into the air after the owl, pecking on her head until she eventually let go of poor Douglas. By this time, they were flying at quite a height, but luckily for Douglas, after a few bumps on branches and a little bit of a rough landing through the leaves, he ended up in the top of an apple tree in the field just beyond the bottom of the garden. Bertie landed in the tree to check on him. Thankfully, he was unharmed, just a bit shaken from the flight and a little dazed from his fall. After a short recovery Douglas was able to climb up onto Bertie's back. Bertie flew him quickly back up to the top of the drainpipe and back into the safety of the loft.

Bertie returned for Anna and Alexander in turn before they were all back safely behind the loft walls. Mr Blackbird was fast asleep in the loft rafters, but Mrs Blackbird, who was wide awake as her chicks were chirping nosily, enquired: "My, whatever happened out there? You all look as though you've had quite a fright!" "We have Mrs Blackbird and it's all my fault!" sobbed Douglas "I was carried off by an owl and Bertie saved my life! How will I ever repay you Bertie?" "It's true Mrs Blackbird that Bertie was incredibly brave," continued Anna whilst giving Douglas a big hug, "I don't know what we would have done without him."

"You're welcome Douglas," cawed Bertie. "Let that be a lesson to you though – the owls in England are just as unfriendly as those in Siberia it seems! The good news is that no harm was done. Now where would you like this hole?"

They all made their way down the wooden beams to the first floor. Here they stopped in a corner above the kitchen. "This should be the perfect place for the new hole Douglas," considered Alexander. "It's in the corner of the kitchen ceiling out of sight from the big people, but it's only about a couple of metres away from the counter where your beloved cheese is stored." "Right then," cawed Bertie as he got himself ready to peck away at the wood and plasterboard, "this shouldn't take long."

Fifteen minutes later a Douglas sized hole had been made in the kitchen ceiling through which they could all see the cheese on the kitchen counter and the mouse traps on the floor below. "This is perfect Bertie. You have done so much for me tonight; I cannot thank you enough," said Douglas. "If there is anything I can ever do to repay you, please do not hesitate to ask me." "Well, it's certainly been an exciting evening!" yawned Bertie, "but I'm not a nocturnal creature like hamsters and field mice are and I need to be out pecking tree bark in search of beetle grubs in a couple of hours. I am going to head off for some sleep. Anna, I will meet you tomorrow evening at half past midnight just outside of the bottom of the drainpipe. You won't need to make the dangerous journey across the patio, but it will mean that you still get to slide down the drainpipe as I know how much you enjoyed that."

Night creatures or not, they all realised that the evening's adventures had made them all very sleepy indeed, so they all said "goodnight" through stifled yawns and wearily headed off to their beds for some well-earned rest.

Chapter 6 – Cheddar Gorge

Anna awoke to the sound of the big people shutting up the house before going upstairs to bed. She yawned and stretched. This evening was the evening that Douglas could finally eat his beloved cheese again. Although she did not need to keep any of her grains for Douglas tonight, she did need to keep some aside for Bertie as payment for making the new hole. As she ate her breakfast, Anna thought that she would keep even more grains aside than originally planned for Bertie as a thank you for saving her good friend's life. It was the least she could do!

After breakfast Anna decided to have another run on her wheel. Looking out at the night sky from The Study window, she gave a little shudder remembering the ordeal with the owl. She doubted that she would ever enjoy listening to them hooting to each other ever again! She focused on watching the bats darting after insects instead.

Running around and around in her wheel, Anna was so lost in her thoughts of the previous night's adventures that she did not hear Douglas knock on her cage door at midnight. Poor Douglas had to knock three times before she was brought back to reality! “Sorry Douglas, I was daydreaming about all of the adventures we’ve had!” explained Anna. “It makes me sad to think that tonight might be our last one, but I might also be pleased for a little peace and quiet for a while,” she pondered. “I’m going to be very pleased to get my cheese back,” agreed Douglas, “but that’s not to say that this will be our last adventure. I will of course still come and visit you.” They gave each other a big hug. Anna filled her cheeks with as many of Bertie’s grains as she could squeeze in whilst still being able to talk without her mouth full. They then set off. Anna now knew exactly which paths to follow along the wooden beams behind the walls. Douglas went off to fetch Tilly and Anna continued zigzagging up and up into the loft.

“Good evening Mr and Mrs Blackbird,” she nodded as she came across their nest. They were busy trying to settle their chicks down for the night. “I’m just popping out to meet Bertie to pay him in grains for the brilliant help he was to Douglas.” “Well, you be careful,” worried Mrs Blackbird, “we don’t want a repeat of last night!” “Oh, most certainly not,” agreed Anna and she went on to explain: “Bertie has kindly offered to meet me on the grass just outside of the drainpipe, so there shouldn’t be any bother from the owls.”

Anna remembered the advice that Douglas had given her about keeping her little pink paws crossed over her chest and her tiny pink feet together, to avoid any potential issues of getting stuck! She once again sat on the lip of the pipe, gave herself a little push, and off she went! Even though she had experienced the slide before, she could not help herself “weeeeeeeee!!!” she shouted as she shot down the pipe, eventually spilling out onto the soft garden grass. As she lay there, she looked up and saw that Bertie was smiling down at her. “I’ll never get tired of such fun,” laughed Anna, “although my cheeks are so full of your grains that I was worried that I might get stuck.” Bertie laughed back. “I don’t have cheeks I can store the grains in, and I don’t want to eat them all in one go, I’ll be too full to fly!” explained Bertie, “but I did find a rose petal that should hold them all, at least long enough for me to carry them back to my nest later.” “Good thinking,” said Anna as she deposited the grains onto the beautiful yellow rose petal. Once done, she climbed onto Bertie’s back and he flew her back up to the top of the drainpipe and into the safety of the loft. She thanked him again for all he had done and promised to stay in contact via Mr Blackbird. After a big hug, she left him talking with Mr and Mrs Blackbird and headed back down the wooden beams to the first floor where Tilly was weaving the most amazing construction she had ever seen!

Douglas and Alexander were leaning back against one of the wooden beams watching in awe as Tilly worked effortlessly. Anna joined them. Within twenty minutes Tilly was finished. She fixed one end of the bridge securely to the beam against which the companions had been leaning. Bundling the rest of the bridge between the back two of her eight legs, she then set off through the new hole in the ceiling. The next task was to spin a guide rope all the way down to the back of the kitchen counter on top of which the cheese was sitting. She was careful to make her creation discreet – to the big people's eyes it was nearly invisible, they might just have glimpsed the bridge if the sunlight reflected off it. When it was complete, she scurried back up to join Anna, Douglas, and Alexander. "Right then my dears," said Tilly proudly, "it's time for Douglas to try it out!"

Douglas had previously experienced how strong Tilly's thread was when she had lowered him and Anna to the ground floor a couple of nights ago. However, after the experiences of last night, it did not stop him from feeling nervous. Anna could see that Douglas was hesitating, so she reassured him: "Just go slowly Douglas, step by step and you'll be fine, you'll see." Douglas did as Anna suggested ... he eased himself onto the steepest part of the bridge and started to make his descent.

Douglas did not know, but he imagined that his experience was equal to what it would be like walking across a big people's rickety rope bridge.

He was crawling along on all fours, moving headfirst, but his motion, along with the fact that the web was exceptionally light, was making the bridge move quite violently from side to side. This, combined with the fact that poor Douglas was hanging from the ceiling at a considerable height above the mouse traps below, meant that he was not enjoying the crossing very much at all! Tilly could see that he was struggling, so she decided to come to the rescue and spin a handrail on either side of the bridge.

Whilst poor Douglas was hanging there, she also added in some reinforcing threads leading up at various points from the bridge back to the ceiling. The new design features meant that the bridge was not only much more stable, but Douglas could also stand up to walk across holding onto the new handrails as he went. “Phew, that’s much better,” sighed Douglas in relief. “Thank you so much Tilly, you are truly a master of web building!” Before he knew it, Douglas had made the journey down onto the kitchen counter and he stood face to face with his beloved cheese!

Chapter 7 – Home Sweet Home

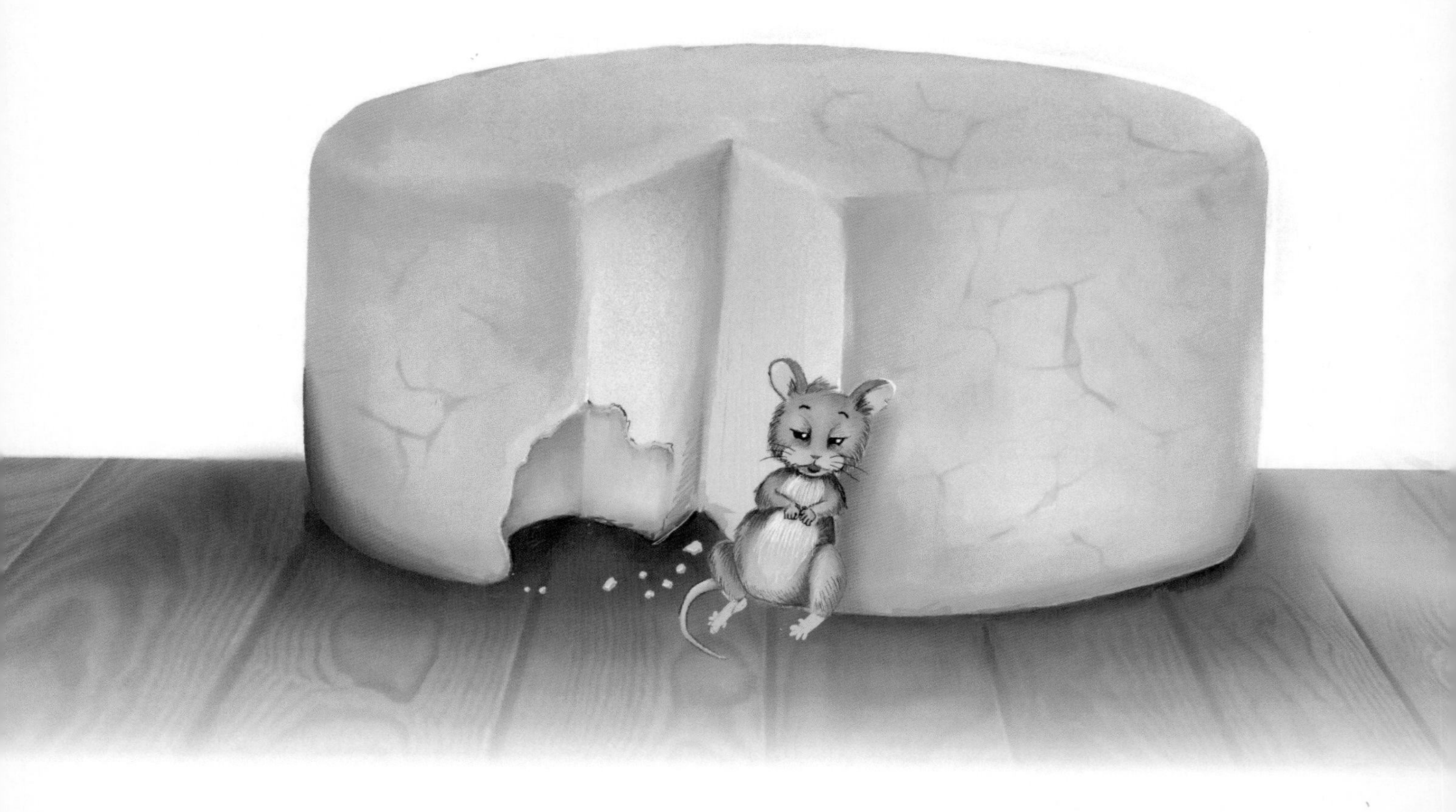

After eating his fill of cheese, Douglas climbed back along the bridge to join his friends. "I can't thank each of you enough for all of the support you've given me over the last few nights," said Douglas with tears in his eyes. "You truly are the best friends a field mouse could ever ask for."

"I can't thank you all enough either," said Anna with tears in her eyes, "I could only dream of the amazing adventures we've shared, and I would never have met you all if the big people hadn't put out those mouse traps."

Then it was Alexander's turn. He surprised them all by saying that the adventures of the last few days had got him longing to have a place to call home again. Douglas had his cosy nest; Tilly had her impressive web and Anna had her cage. Without any hesitation, Anna took both of Alexander's little pink paws in her own and declared "You'll come and live with me Alexander! We have got so much in common. We can sleep and run on the wheel and eat grains whilst reminiscing about all of the adventures we've shared!" "That's so truly kind of you Anna," sniffed Alexander, who by now also had tears in his eyes, "I don't know what to say?" "Say yes!" exclaimed Anna, jumping up and down on the spot in her excitement.

"Oh, how utterly lovely my dears," beamed Tilly, "I do so very much love a happy ending."

And happy they all were. Anna's nest was so fluffy that it was plenty big enough for Alexander to have his own bedroom. The big people could not understand where a second pet hamster had suddenly appeared from, but Alexander was no

bother to look after and the smaller of the big people loved how cuddly he was. Likewise, the big people could equally not understand how the cheddar cheese was still disappearing, despite the traps remaining next to the hole in the kitchen wall!

Douglas continued to visit Anna and Alexander. Sometimes he would enjoy visiting their cage where they would all sit and share a meal of grains and cheese before he would have a go at running on their wheel. Other times he would open the cage door for them so that they could enjoy a visit behind the walls. They would spend time with Tilly or go up to the loft to see Mr and Mrs Blackbird.

The Blackbird chicks were growing up fast. Sometimes, to give Mr and Mrs Blackbird a rest, Anna would babysit the chicks. She would tuck them up in their nest ready to go to sleep and Anna would share stories of her adventures - just as Mother had done with her. The chicks, determined not to go to sleep so that they could listen to more stories, would chirp their excitement of growing up and leaving the nest in the loft. "When we are old enough to fly," they would chirp to Anna, "we are going to take you, Douglas and Alexander on our backs to visit Bertie!"

"I've only flown once," explained Anna, "and that was when Bertie flew me back up to the loft. I have often watched the owls and bats flying and imagined the places they get to visit in a single night. What an amazing adventure that would be!"

It was settled.

A new adventure was waiting, and Anna had her friends to enjoy it with.

The End

Printed in Great Britain
by Amazon